The
Christmas
Journey

Also by Donna VanLiere

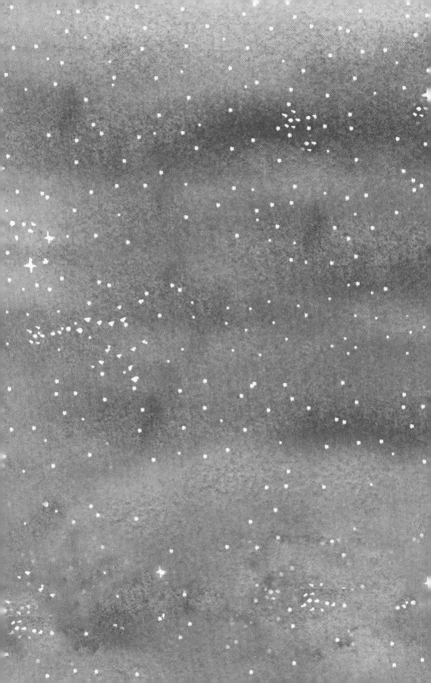

Donna VanLiere

The Christmas Journey

Illustrations by Michael Storrings

St. Martin's Press
New York

www.stmartins.com

Interior design by Kathryn Parise
Illustrations copyright © 2010 by Michael Storrings

ISBN 978-0-312-61372-3

First Edition: November 2010

10 9 8 7 6 5 4 3 2

For Edith "Dee Dee" MacDonald,
who is the purest soul I've ever known

Acknowledgments

Michael Storrings for the beautiful artwork. Your talents run in excess.

Jennifer Gates and Esmond Harmsworth for keeping the book alive, and Jen Enderlin for your enthusiasm.

Mary Weekly for her help and kindness beyond measure.

Troy, Gracie, Kate, and David for keeping the wonderment in Christmas!

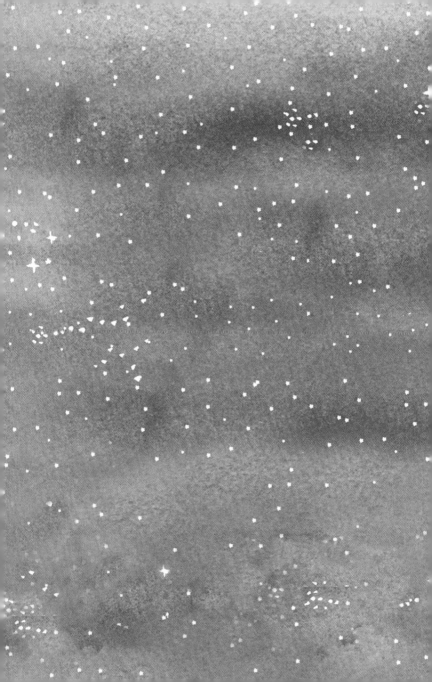

Preface

FROM LUKE 2:1 20

In those days Caesar Augustus issued a decree that a census should be taken of the entire Roman world. (This was the first census that took place while Quirinius was governor of Syria.) And everyone went to his own town to register.

So $Joseph$ $also$ went up from the town of Nazareth in Galilee to Judea, to Bethlehem the town of David, because he belonged to the house and line of David. He went there to register with Mary, who was pledged to be married to him and was expecting a child. While they were there, the time came for the baby to be born, and she gave birth to her firstborn, a son. She wrapped him in cloths and placed him in a manger, because there was no room for them in the inn.

And there were shepherds living out in the fields nearby, keeping watch over their flocks at night. An angel of the Lord appeared to them, and the glory of the Lord shone around them, and they were terrified.

$\mathcal{B}ut\ the\ angel$ said to them, "Do not be afraid. I bring you good news of great joy that will be for all the people. Today in the town of David a Savior has been born to you; he is Christ the Lord. This will be a sign to you: You will find a baby wrapped in cloths and lying in a manger."

Suddenly a great company of the heavenly host appeared with the angel, praising God and saying, "Glory to God in the highest, and on earth peace to men on whom his favor rests."

When the angels had left them and gone into heaven, the shepherds said to one another, "Let's go to Bethlehem and see this thing that has happened, which the Lord has told us about."

$\mathcal{S}o$ *they hurried* off and found Mary and Joseph, and the baby, who was lying in the manger. When they had seen him, they spread the word concerning what had been told them about this child, and all who heard it were amazed at what the shepherds said to them. But Mary treasured up all these things and pondered them in her heart. The shepherds returned,

glorifying and praising God for all the things they had heard and seen, which were just as they had been told.

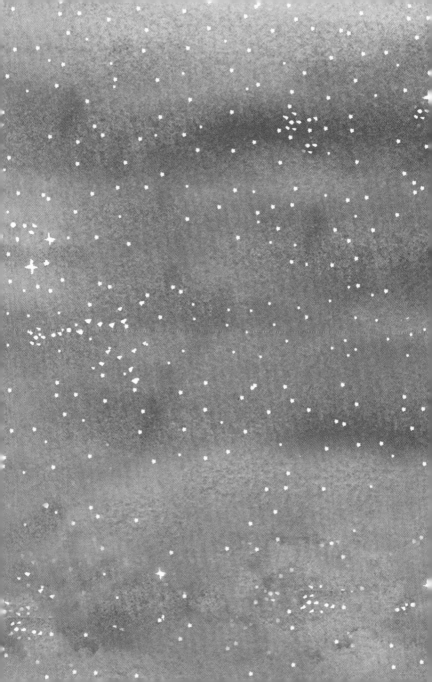

Introduction

The story of the manger scene is familiar to most of us . . . sweet little lambs looking over Jesus, doe-eyed cows and camels standing nearby gazing at the little Christ child, Mary and Joseph snuggled warmly together admiring the baby comfortable in his soft bed of hay, wise men and shepherds gathering to worship and giving gifts to the King in the warm, well lit stable, and always that magnificent star above to show the way. At least that's the image greeting card companies and church pageants have painted over the years. Somewhere along the way the cave has been sanitized, the birth made painless, and the people involved stripped of all fear or emotion. It seems we have colored in or forgotten much of what happened to make that journey possible.

Christmas today is a full-blown industry. Muzak fills malls and grocery stores with "Winter Wonderland" and "The Little Drummer Boy" before the Thanksgiving turkey is picked off the bone. Bell ringers take their places earlier each year and meteorologists forecast the mildest day to do that last-minute shopping. Cards with the scribbled signature of someone you vaguely know in the family tree cram your mailbox, and on TV a big-haired woman wearing an impish elf skirt and Santa hat sits on the side of a hot tub and invites you to buy one today at rock-bottom Christmas prices. Where has the wonderment gone? Where is the sense that

one plus one somehow no longer equal two but add up to a million on that dazzling, holy, and remarkable day?

I wrote this several years ago for a church Christmas banquet. I read it as a narrative then, as a reminder, and still do today. I hope you will do the same . . . so you won't forget.

The Christmas Journey

They have to go. They have no choice. Emperor Caesar Augustus has issued a decree that a census will be taken of the entire Roman world to aid in military drafting and tax collection. Although the Jews do not have to serve in the Roman army, but since they are obligated to pay

1

taxes to Rome, everyone will have to go and register at the place of their ancestral home. For Joseph's family it would be over seventy miles and a four-to-seven-day walk from Nazareth to Bethlehem, the town of his ancestors. It's not going to be an easy journey either, considering the shape Mary is in. She is nine months pregnant and will have to make the trip that winds through wilderness, desert, and mountainside, sitting sidesaddle on a donkey and feeling every rock and bump along the way.

Joseph leads the donkey out of the village at dawn. Mary's eyes are heavy, but he spent a sleepless night and has been awake for hours waiting for light. The smell of fish and eggs cooking on morning fires saturates the street with a misty fog as families prepare for breakfast. Joseph's stomach rumbles as he packs the donkey. He should have eaten more but is anxious to get on the road. His eyes meet Mary's as he helps her onto the donkey. He nods and she smiles in the half-light. Joseph walks beside the donkey, and although he does not look at them, he feels the eyes of his neighbors as they pass. The chattering of three women drawing water ceases as he and Mary go by, and Mary keeps her head down. She has long known what they think of her. The laughter of two men mending a fishing net subsides to a whisper as the donkey approaches, and children stop playing in the street when their mothers clack their tongues and snap their fingers.

Joseph sets his jaw and ignores them, relieved to get away for a while. The angel of God had visited him and Mary about this baby, but he hadn't visited everyone in town. Joseph has heard the townspeople ridicule Mary. He has seen them point and then turn away, ostracizing her with their clenched teeth and cold shoulders. "Perversion," they have said. "Prostituted under the nose of her father." The gossiped indictments and whispered innuendoes have seeped under every doorway. The conception was not cloaked in anonymity. Everyone knew her name. They knew her father and mother's name.

Joseph's own heart has throbbed with a dull pain for weeks, and looking at Mary, he wonders how someone so young is able to bear the burden of such a stigma.

Mary lays her hands on her swollen belly. The baby dropped into the birth canal days ago, causing increasing discomfort. A chill clings to the shadows that stretch over the sleepy town, and Joseph places a thin blanket over Mary's legs. The morning echoes grow distant as they thread their way out of town, and Joseph's tensions ease.

"*Are you well?*" he asks.

"*I am*," she says, smiling, rubbing her stomach. "He is no longer stirring but is heavy inside."

Joseph forces a smile and quickens his steps. What if she gives birth on the side of a mountain? What if the baby comes in the middle of the wilderness? What would he do? Who could help him? Several families from Nazareth are traveling in caravans on the road ahead and behind them, but Joseph does not feel he can rely on them for help. He has never felt so isolated in his life.

They are quiet as the sun rises. There is so much to discuss, so many questions to ask, but neither of them is ready. Thoughts swirl in their minds as the donkey clop-clops his way over the terrain. The valley is a canvas of windblown grass swimming with wildflowers and fruit trees. Mary does not pick any fruit yet; there would be more opportunities on the journey. The smell of balsam fills the air, and Mary takes a deep breath, the scent reminding her of childhood playtime on the hills surrounding her home.

The road ahead is full of twists and turns as lush valley turns to chalky dirt and then rock. Mary is jostled about on the donkey, and a flashing pain takes her breath. She reaches for her back, attempting to ease the hurt, but there it is again. She leans forward on the donkey and holds her breath till the ache passes. It seems so long ago that she was baking bread in her home, a young girl giggling with her mother and teasing her siblings. Was it only nine months ago? Mary smiles, her mind swirling with sweet childlike noises from her parent's home.

She moves her hand over her abdomen. There was no longer a plate set for her at her parent's table. Her place of rest beside her sister was now empty. They would no longer whisper into the night, sharing girlish secrets and stories. She closes her eyes and breathes deeply. It is still too much to comprehend that the promise of God is enfleshed in her womb, dependent upon her for life.

In a small village, Joseph helps Mary to the ground, where women are picking over fruit in the marketplace. He leads the donkey to a trough filled with water. Mary stretches and arches her back. "Are you hungry?" she asks.

"Always," Joseph says, taking off his sandals.

She unwraps some bread and fish she brought from home. These foods always travel well, and she hopes she has packed enough for their trip. She reaches into a satchel for some figs and a pomegranate they picked out-

side the village.

"*Do you want* to sit?" he asks, pointing to the shade of a tree.

"*No*," *she says*, laughing. He sits beneath the tree and pushes the bread into his mouth. Mary walks to the well in the center of town and draws water, filling a cup and taking it to Joseph. He drinks it down and she fills it again. She hands the cup to him and leans against the tree. The noise of customers haggling over prices and the clanking of merchandise in the marketplace drifts on the wind as

Mary watches the donkey drink. "Are you frightened, Joseph?" she asks.

He looks up at her. Every illusion he had of starting a family with her ended months ago when she told him she was pregnant. Every conceivable dream of the village celebrating their wedding shattered when rumors swelled that his betrothed was a harlot. Swept away with those dreams were his plans and desires and every expectation he had for their new life together. He was torn from the privacy of a once-quiet life and shifted

17

into one of public shame and ridicule. He is still trying to wrap his mind around all that has taken place in so short a time. He watches Mary as the corners of her mouth turn up in soft edges. For months now, those she has grown up with, who have shared meals around her family's table have been quick to brand her, but these well-mannered guardians of morality never even cupped their ear to hear the truth or offered a word of compassion. The hourglass has been turned and eternity is fast approaching, but their thoughts have been consumed with how the law of Moses is unwavering concerning what to do with those caught in sexual sin. The very angel who came to Mary all those months ago must surely have guarded her life from the hatred and condemnation of the righteous bent on vengeance in the name of God. How else has her life been spared? Is she frightened? He cannot tell. He hasn't known her long enough to discern her emotions or fears. They are both so new to each other.

"The angel told me not to be afraid," he says.

A breeze laps at her face and she remains quiet, thinking. "So then, you are not?"

He breaks the bread in two and hands her a piece. "I wish I could say that I am not, but I am. I am terrified." He watches as others gather around the well. "What does that make me?"

S*he sits on* the ground and reaches for a fig. "As human as I," she says. "I too am frightened. There is so much that I don't know." Her voice is faint. "So much that I will never understand." He looks at her, and her eyes are deep, touching the far reaches of her soul. "Why was I chosen for this? Why you?"

He shakes his head. "How will I teach him?"

"How do you teach any child?" she asks.

He turns his face to her. "Yes. But how do you teach *him*?" They eat in silence as the question fills the air around them. "How will I raise him?"

"With love," she says.

He looks at her. "But is love from a common man enough?"

She traces her finger through the blades of grass in front of her. "It will be more than enough," she says. "It is the very reason he's coming."

Their rest is short; they want to make the next town by nightfall. The donkey's footing is unsure beneath Mary on the mountainside, and she urges Joseph to stop and help her to the ground. Her breath is shallow as she walks behind Joseph; she hasn't been able to take a deep breath in weeks. Her legs begin to cramp, and she stumbles over rocks on the path, groping for the donkey's back. "Joseph, stop!" she says, catching her breath. "I can't go on." Joseph helps her sit on a rock protruding from the mountain. She wipes her forehead and pushes her hand over her belly; it is hard and no longer seems to be part of her. She winces at the pain of an early contraction, and Joseph loosens the straps of her sandals, slipping them off her swollen feet. He brushes caked dirt away from her toes and ankles.

She groans and rests her head against the mountain, gasping for air. There are no royal privileges for this birth—no attendants to help them over the mountain, no cooks to tend their meals or servants to soothe her aching back and feet. This baby would not be born into a soft-cushioned life. A pain knifes through her again and she screams. Tears fill her eyes, and when Joseph sees her tears, every thought that has occupied his mind on the journey flees. He pulls her head onto his shoulder, holding her till the hurt subsides. "He will come soon," Mary says between breaths. Joseph feels his heart race and he nods.

It is late on the fifth day when they reach Bethlehem. The town is already crowded from the many pilgrims traveling for the census, all of them clamoring for a place to stay.

The westering sun breathes a final sigh, escaping with the last glints of light. Joseph's nerves are on edge as he seeks lodging. His feet are blistered and sore and Mary is exhausted. The contractions started growing closer together hours ago, and she is nearing the end of her strength. Mary is jostled and bumped as Joseph inches his way through the congested street. The crush of the crowd pushes them forward at a pace that frightens Mary.

People are bustling outside the inn, and Joseph leaves her alone on the donkey as he presses his way to the door.

$\mathcal{A}$ *beggar reaches* for Joseph's arm, but someone pushes the old man out of the way. Joseph raps on the door and can hear commotion behind it. He knocks louder, and a harried man with a pale face opens the door.

"There is no room," he says, before Joseph can speak. Joseph peers around him and sees that the inn is so bloated with people that some are lying on the floor or curled up on the stairs. The innkeeper and Joseph stare at each other in clumsy silence before Joseph thanks him and turns to leave, shaking his head at Mary. Her face is stricken as she holds her stomach. Her water has broken, and it won't be long before the baby comes.

"You," the innkeeper says. Joseph turns to look at him. "You can stay there," the innkeeper says, pointing to his stable in the hillside. "My guests' animals are inside, but if you can find a space among them, you are welcome to it."

Joseph surveys the busy street and realizes there is no place for them to go. He looks at Mary and she nods; they have no other option. "Thank you. We'll take it," he tells the innkeeper.

When Joseph opens the stable door, the stench of hot, sweaty animals and manure assaults them. He hesitates for a moment—this is no place for a birth—but Mary groans, her face twisting in agony.

Joseph helps her off the donkey and holds an oil lamp the innkeeper has given them to guide Mary into the stable.

The darkened barn frightens him; Mary might stumble and fall. The lamp he carries is barely enough light to read by let alone usher in the birth of the Christ child.

Sheep scatter throughout the stable as he leads Mary inside; a disgruntled cow stamps her foot and lifts her tail to urinate. Donkeys kick at the stable wall and bray, their breath coming out in puffy clouds of mist.

$\mathcal{J}oseph$ *spots an* empty space against the back wall that will have to serve as the birthing room. Mary can rest there. He helps her to the floor, and she leans her head against the earthen wall, her back aching from carrying the weight of the world in her womb. This is a dismal place for a woman no older than a child to give birth to a child. She hadn't imagined this pain when she told the angel she was the Lord's servant.

"*May it be* to me as you have said," she had told him.

She moans; the contractions are growing closer together now. Outside, the shadows grow still and deepen more as the agony of life awakens the night.

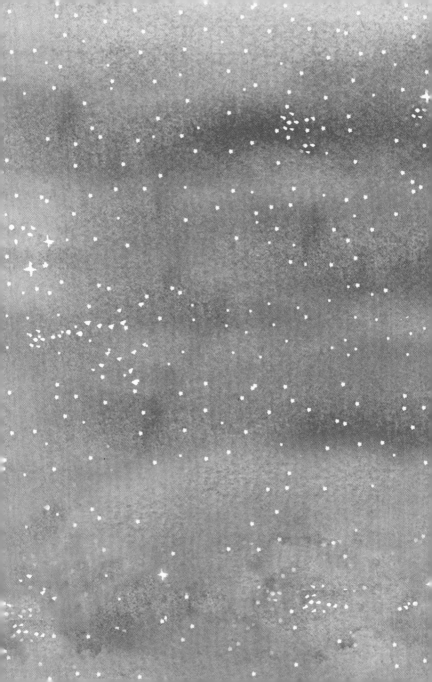

As Joseph tries to keep the oil lamp lit, Mary grabs his hand. "Joseph, hurry! Find what you can." Grabbing the lamp, he leaves Mary alone in the darkness. He stumbles through the stable and spots a trough that could serve as a bed, and the hay that the sheep are sleeping on could do as bedding—but there are no blankets!

He whirls around, searching the pens and walls. What can he use for blankets? His robe would have to work for now. He pulls it off as a contraction seizes Mary. Her scream pierces the night. "Joseph, I need you! Please, Joseph! Hurry!" She tries to pull herself upright in a squatting position, but her legs tremble beneath her, forcing her on her back.

Another scream brings Joseph running from the watering trough, cold water spilling over the bucket rim. The Light of the World pushes his way into the darkness as Joseph rushes to help. As he sets the lamp down, Joseph's heart pounds with uncertainty and his hands tremble. He has seen the birth of many animals but never that of a child. Mary cries and pushes her elbows into the ground. She grabs at dirt, straw, anything she can clutch in her hands. Joseph coaches as best he knows how: wiping

sweat from her brow and guiding the baby out, but Mary is tired; her strength is nearly gone. "Can you push again?" Joseph asks, holding the baby's head in his hands.

She shakes her head. "I cannot," she screams. Her hair sticks to the perspiration on her face, and streams of sweat pour over her neck and chest.

"You must," he pleads. "You must try!"

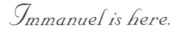

She pushes with what seems to be little result, her cries rising above those of the animals. Joseph urges her to keep pushing, keep pushing. And with one final cry of anguish and a push, her labor is over.

Immanuel is here.

His skin is light. The olive color would appear slowly in the weeks to come. His head is misshapen from being pushed through the birth canal. His body is red, blotchy, covered with mucus. Is this truly the Son of the Almighty God, screaming now as his earthly father smacks his bottom? Joseph uses some of the animals' rags and wipes off the slippery fluid, then swaddles the baby in dry ones. Mary lies on the stable floor, trying to catch her breath. The Messiah's cries are louder now.

$\mathcal{M}$ary reaches for her newborn, and Joseph clumsily hands him to her. "Shh, shh, shh," she says, laying him on her chest and guiding his tiny head to find what he is looking for. Is this the same voice that had spoken the world into existence . . . whimpering now at the breast of a maidservant? Mary caresses his face and counts each finger on his tiny hand. And hands that once placed the stars in the sky and sculpted magnificent landscapes grasp her finger. Mary secrets away each movement and sound and scent in her heart. He looks up, and eyes that saw her before she was born strain to see his mother. She laughs as his tiny mouth turns up into a slight crescent. The face of God smiling. Mary kisses his forehead and holds him closer. Deity swaddled in the arms of humanity.

Joseph sits in the silence and watches. His face is weathered and flushed. There was a time, at the beginning of the pregnancy that he wanted to walk away. But after the angel spoke with him, he knew he should stay, and now, looking at his wife and son, the depths of his heart swell to the surface and his eyes blur. This is *he* of whom the prophets spoke, seeking nourishment from his mother. Stretching before them is a new life, together as a family, filled with first words, first laughs, and first steps. He would teach his son how to plane a piece of wood and hold a hammer, just as his father had taught him. God's Son would grow up with the smell of sawdust in his nostrils. Joseph's chest pounds with the wonder and mystery of it all. He comes closer, holding Mary in his arms, and together they look at this baby . . . Jesus, who opens his mouth in a yawn.

The Savior is sleepy.

In an incomprehensible, humbling move, the Son of God left the majestic splendor of heaven and stepped down into our world to become an infant, to become a man. There were no royal robes or parades, no trumpeted arrival. At a birth where there should have been the finest marble and linens, there was only dirt, a few bales of hay, and the filthy rags of animals. Where there should have been a legion of angels, there was just a handful of bleating sheep, a couple of anxious camels, and a few tethered donkeys. And where there should have been a king and a queen and the pomp and circumstance of a royal court, there was only a frightened teenager and her tradesman spouse. Angels did announce the birth of the King but only to a few shepherds guarding their flocks. And that brilliant star was shining in the night; but with the exception of three foreigners, no one even bothered to notice it.

And so, in that little town of Bethlehem so long ago, a simple peasant girl and her carpenter husband quietly sang lullabies to the King of kings as he drifted off to sleep.